LET'S READ WITH MAX AND KATE

PLAYTIME

with Max and Kate

MICK MANNING

PowerKiDS press™

NEW YORK

Published in 2018 by The Rosen Publishing Group, Inc.
29 East 21st Street, New York, NY 10010

Written by Mick Manning
Illustrated by Brita Granström
Compiled by Joanne Randolph

Book Design: Sarah Liddell
Editor: Joanne Randolph

Cataloging-in-Publication Data

Names: Manning, Mick.
Title: Playtime with Max and Kate / Mick Manning.
Description: New York : PowerKids Press, 2018. | Series: Let's read with Max and Kate| Includes index.
Identifiers: LCCN ISBN 9781538340745 (pbk.) | ISBN 9781538340738 (library bound) | ISBN 9781538340752 (6 pack)
Subjects: LCSH: Play–Juvenile fiction. | Games–Juvenile fiction.
Classification: LCC PZ7.M345 Pl 2018 | DDC [E]–dc23

Manufactured in the United States of America

CPSIA Compliance Information: Batch #CS18PK: For Further Information contact Rosen Publishing, New York, New York at 1-800-237-9932

CONTENTS

Max and Kate are playing soccer.
Charlie wants to play, too.

Oops! Charlie picks up the soccer ball and runs into the goal!

"Here, Charlie, I'll show you how to play," says Kate. She kicks the ball like a pro, and Max claps.

Now it's Max's turn! The ball
sails over everyone's head and
into the pond!

Kate hoots with laughter.
"Max, the ducks don't want
to play soccer with us!"

Max and Kate are playing a
game called Hungry Coyote.
Cowboy Max is sleeping by
his campfire, guarding his
cheese crackers.

9

Kate is the hungry coyote. She must creep across the room and steal a cracker without making a sound.

If Cowboy Max wakes up, then
Coyote Kate has to start all
over again!

Max listens for the smallest sound.
Kate moves silently, just like a
real coyote.

Suddenly—*crunch!* Kate munches
a cracker loudly. "Well, Cowboy,"
she chuckles. "It's your turn to be
Coyote now."

MAX AND KATE PLAY WITH ICE

Max and Kate are playing outside with Mo, Kiwi, and Kate's dolls.

She finds a plastic tray and fills
it with water. "What's that for?"
asks Max. "You'll see," grins Kate.

They leave the tray and go inside
for some hot chocolate.

Later Max sees that the water
in the tray has frozen solid.
"Don't worry," he says. "The ice
will melt soon."

"No, I want it like that," chuckles Kate. "It's an ice-skating rink for my dolls!" Max laughs, too, and zooms a doll over the ice.

18

Come one, come all! It's Maxie
and Katy, the world's greatest,
most magical team!

Max pulls Mo out of a top hat.
"Abracadabra and presto!"
he shouts. The audience cheers.

Next, Kate juggles two oranges
while balancing Kiwi on her
head. "Let's hear it for the
amazing Katy!" Max says.

"Now it's time for milk and cookies, everyone," says Kate's mommy. "Oh no! Where did the cookies go?" asks Max.

"Charlie is a magician, too,"
chuckles Kate. "He made the
cookies disappear."

QUESTIONS TO THINK ABOUT

- What types of games do Max and Kate play?

- Games usually have rules. What are some of the rules in the games Max and Kate play? What's one rule for soccer? What's a rule for the Hungry Coyote game?

- Some games we play are games we make up using our imaginations. Have you ever made up a game? Which game that Max and Kate play would you most like to play?

INDEX